Journey
to
Empycrist II.

JOURNEY TO EMPYCRIST II

First edition. June 2, 2024.

Copyright © 2024 Laurent Sueur.

ISBN: 979-8223691884

Written by Laurent Sueur.

Table of Contents

Chapter 1:
Obviousness.

The universe, as far as we can judge from our poor knowledge and perception, is characterized by an absence of colour. Everything works as if black, or at least a very dark blue, were to be the dominant impression, sometimes contradicted by the platinum scintillation of the celestial bodies. In the Solar System, we are blessed since we have Mars, with its reddish reflection, our gorgeous gold sun and, of course, the aquamarine-like Earth. The Earth, so heavenly beautiful, so unbearably offended by the human vermin! Are you dying? It seems so! It is impossible: it is the Creator's chef d'oeuvre, the epitome of perfection. However, over the years, its empyreal blue has faded and air pollution has put a yellowish veil between the crystalline depths of its oceans and the mesosphere. It is unbelievable! The titanic collisions this planet experienced did not destroy it, and, man, this minuscule creature, could achieve what the immense universe was unable to fulfil. Would collective unconsciousness be stronger than celestial geometry?

Planet Earth is suffocating, for mankind had no other choice but to burn fossil fuels and release the venom that will kill it. Bad luck! Another technology would have induced a better present. Bad luck? No, bad attitude of mind: they would have caused a lot of other problems, just for the pleasure of devouring themselves. Ordinary people are ogres! Their doubtful normalcy is the tip of their mental iceberg. What can we find underneath? Barbarity: all the vices they have consciously chosen before reaching a state of pure madness, the insanity of normality. Ah, where are you, reason and grace? Elsewhere, undoubtedly: in the mind of an exceptional soul, on the surface of another planet, in the logic of humane human organizations...

Their air is polluted, they have no more energy resources, and, now, they also have problems with water supply! It has to be said that global warming was a two-faced birthday present. Of course, it brought some water where it has disappeared, but, at the same time, it brought a lot of water where there was already too much. Hence, some deserts with low population densities became livable places while most of the overcrowded parts of the world flooded. Henceforth, crops and fruit trees were destroyed, and stagnant water caused large epidemics, as usual. Very few places were spared: some drylands of the center of the United States, China and Africa. Sunny California, what do you prefer: pestilential water or the hellish reality of your burning thirst?

With fewer people on the planet, the many mistakes of man would have never led to such a disaster. Actually, 350 million must be the appropriate number of inhabitants: 8 billion is absurd. There is not enough quantity of renewable energy for so many people, even though it is not completely impossible to produce a sufficient amount of food. Moreover, since barbarity is included in human nature, one must let them spread out. They must not gather together if their level of consciousness is too low, or else they would endanger themselves and even try to kill one another. Barbarity must not be societies' fate.

THE INVICTUS IS ABOUT to lift off. The spaceship is massive. It looks like a gigantic albatross shining under the imperious sun of Port Isabel. The weather is fine today and the sky is rather blue; no, it is rather... yellow! Captain Smith is nervous, not because of the danger of the liftoff, but because he thinks that the die is cast. All his hopes have vanished: he is here today, for he must find another planet so that the human race may survive and, perhaps, start all over again. John, you are so sad. Your grief and the bottomless abyss of your regrets are palpable. You can hardly breathe; you are quiet... Are you shivering?

Barbara is next to him. She is thinking about her chimpanzees: they are sedated. So, they won't see anything, shout, or try to escape, like the last time. She really cares about them, for she is certain that they will help her to understand, at last, why they are so different from humans, although they have almost the same genetic material and physical characteristics. She has been working with them for the last 5 years and has taught them how to speak! Well, it is clear that they understand some words, but I would not say they really communicate with her, nor with one another. Were the first hominins like them? When did they start to speak? Why? And what was the first word ever spoken? God, sun, water, earth? Oh, no! It was I... am!

Peter is also a biologist: he studies the plant kingdom. You should see what he has done in the greenhouse of the Invictus: it is the Garden of Eden. It is even better since there are no snakes, no Adam, no Eve, and no fallen angels. But the Tree of the knowledge of good and evil must be there: he has planted so many different species. Couldn't he rather look for the Tree of the knowledge of the place of man in the universe? Everything has a place, a function and therefore a meaning. However, it seems that the place of man fluctuates or, at least, is not really understandable. Indeed, he is an element of the gigantic motion. The wasps once made him understand that he was someone really special. Actually, these small creatures always eat the fruit borne by his trees before he does: they make a little hole, which attracts other insects like the ants. In next to no time, the fruit is eaten by them. Last year, for the very first time, they did not touch the peaches. Why? He does not know. What he knows is that, without him, animals and humans would starve and disappear...

The brunette seated opposite him is Jenny. She is a linguist. She understands and even speaks many different languages, which could be useful if they found intelligent living beings on Empycrist II. She is not really convinced by that, because it is almost certain that they will not speak Chinese, nor... Latin! It is strange: the very same object, or idea, always produces many different idiomatic results. It is strange because, from a physical point of view, all humans have the same larynx and brain; so, why don't they use the same sounds to call that object? Matter does not explain everything: matter explains nothing, indeed!

As for Paul, who is seated next to her, he is an astrophysicist or a poet; well, it is the same! He is the most intelligent one of them all, a wise man who is mesmerized by the existence of everything, including himself. He would like to know the starting point of the universe and the reason for its existence. Nothingness does not exist: this overcrowded Creation comes from "something". He thinks that before the beginning of this "something", there was a thought, with its own logic, that created the universal motion. The planetary motion is therefore the reflection of the motion of the primordial will. This heavenly geometry reveals its essence, which is perfection. This cyclopean symmetry leads to man, the only creature that does not always reach its nature. It can also alter other creatures, like Barbara's apes. Man, with his imperfections, can consciously choose his destiny, refuse to follow the logic of perfection and remain in a state of pure barbarity...

Test director.
-How do you feel, John?
John.
-... Bad, really bad.
Test director.
-... 20 minutes before liftoff.
John.
-... Everything seems OK.
Test director.
-You know how important
your mission is?
John.
-Unfortunately! And I still think it is
a stupid idea to go to this planet and
organize a great migration.
The problem is not the planet,
it is the people who live on it.
Give them another one
and they will destroy it.
Barbara.
-John, if I may be so bold,
it is not our responsibility to decide
whether it is a good or a bad idea.
We must obey: that's it!
John.
-Whom must I obey, what must I follow?
Test director.
-I got a short message
from the president...
Jenny, Peter and Paul.

JOURNEY TO EMPYCRIST II

-Oh no...
John.
-Change the subject, and thank him
for all he has not done!
Test director.
-... 9 minutes before liftoff.
John.
-Flight recorders on.
Paul.
-John, you are not the only person who is upset.
We are all regretful.
Things could have been different, but
the reason and humanity of a few
are powerless against the thoughtlessness
of the majority of people.
Peter.
-Consciousness can always escape.
Jenny.
-That's what we are doing.
Test director.
-5 minutes before liftoff.
Connections removed.
Barbara.
-What will we find?
We know what we leave behind,
but what will we find?
Peter.
-The Garden of Eden. I hope so.
Jenny.
-Something better. Look at the Earth.
It is unbearable here.
Paul.
-Solitude, obviously.
Jenny.
-What do you mean by that?

Paul.
-Man is the only intelligent creature
in the endless universe.
Jenny.
-Empycrist II is Earth's twin sister,
why wouldn't we find
intelligent living beings on its surface?
Paul.
-Because man is the aim of the Creation.
He is the result of a decision, not of
the implementation of material factors.
Test director.
-2 minutes before takeoff.
Main engine on.
Barbara.
-... Will we find almond trees
on Empycrist?
Peter.
-No, I don't think so.
Barbara.
-I like to see them bloom in February
while nature is still asleep.
Paul, Jenny and John.
-So do I.
Paul.
-But the sun will be brighter
where we go...
Test director.
-6 seconds... main engine:
maximum power.
Paul.
-Farewell Hell!
Test director.
-Liftoff.
John.

JOURNEY TO EMPYCRIST II

-Hello, Heaven!

Chapter 2:
The Invictus.

The Invictus is a modern cathedral: it is massive, dark and silent. The real captain is the computer, for the engineers did not trust man's emotionally-influenced intelligence. Hence, artificial intelligence handles everything. One would even wonder whether there are not too many people in this expedition! Well, since the journey will last one year, at least five people are required to break the monotony of an endless odyssey. Each day might look like the day before. Some of them will be busier than the others. It is self-evident that Jenny, Paul and John won't be very active, that Peter will take care of the greenhouse, even though everything is automated, and that Barbara will keep on working on her apes. The rhythm of the days will follow the beat of their stomachs! At the moment, everybody is going to their cabins without thinking about their forthcoming boredom.

Barbara's cabin is really pretty. It looks like an 18th century boudoir, but where is Madame de Pompadour? It might be her! Although she is fifty, she is still attractive: cosmetic surgery can easily erase the traces of time, whereas philosophy, or psychoanalysis, is not as efficient as it regarding the way to turn old little girls into grownups. She is lying on her bed, wearing a blue negligee. She is thinking. She is confused because of the monkeys, the almond trees, her husband, Empycrist, her solitude, and the absence of children. She would have liked to have children; she tried... She failed! Life was unfair to her. She would have liked to be a mum. You could have become a woman... Unfruitful flowers turn into fragile old little girls sometimes. If it is not your fault, Barbara, it is your Greek tragedy. This way, you would have understood what humanity means. You would have realized that what resembles you is not you. You would have experienced the passing of time, which tells you that you must hurry up, define what the goal of human life is, follow your human nature, accomplish what you have to do, and turn the ugly worm into a beautiful butterfly before you die. With a child, you would have created. Matter is not everything: it is what you see, it is not what you feel. Barbara, can you create? The love two individuals share must move them to confirm the union of their volition. When a woman mothers a child, she gives birth to a soul. Matters disappears; the mind imposes the brightness of its truth. Barbara, you cannot think yet!

She is facing a mirror. She does not see herself. Her empty gaze is diving into her empty life. Her eyes are wide open. She is parting her curly blond hair. She must pretty herself up for tonight's meeting. She is sighing. Don't put too much mascara on your eyelashes, nor too much rouge on your cheeks and lips: you are not the Evil Queen, for you know that you are not the fairest one of all. There is no need to take your daughter-in-law's heart: you don't hate her! You are crying. Do you know why? Humans' distress always turns them into less unpleasant living beings, but it never turns them into more compassionate creatures. Do you understand yourself? No, you cannot because you first need to become a grownup and stop believing that you are the center of the universe. If you want to see you as you are, you need to move away from yourself. Don't put too much perfume, for you could inconvenience the captain. Moreover, there is no man to seduce. Put this little grey uniform on. It is decent, convenient, and not too feminine. You don't need to look like a femme fatale: don't try to pretend that you are someone you are not. You will only fool yourself. They will immediately understand who you are by the way you talk. The look and the semblance of truth are revealed by the emptiness of the words. Don't pretend that you are a woman, Barbara, for you are still a little girl, and they know it.

John.
-We must talk seriously about
the nature of this mission.
Paul.
-Is it really necessary?
We know the reason and the destination.
John.

-We know the reason and destination,
but we don't know whether it is
a good idea to go there
and organize a mass migration.
Paul.
-What do you mean by that?
Jenny.
-John is planning a kind of mutiny!
We have just left the Earth and you are
already questioning the mission!
Peter.
-But John is right: we are not obliged
to follow an idea when it is a stupid idea.
We are not obedient slaves.
Port Isabel control team rarely
tells the truth.
Barbara.
-You, plotters!
Paul.
-Barbara is right:
we must help mankind to survive.
Barbara.
-We are too weak, too small:
we must obey their orders.
John.
-It is not a question of being big or small, or
obedient or disobedient; it is a matter of logic. It is completely absurd to give
another planet to humans: they will also destroy it. The problem is not
geography but mankind. Honestly, you should find another one each
millennium. There are not so many viable planets in the universe.
So, man must learn to deal with
what he has received and nothing else.
Temperance should be
the first virtue of societies.
Jenny.

JOURNEY TO EMPYCRIST II

So, we go there, fake our own death in a so-called crash, and hope that they
won't send another mission, not to rescue us but to
achieve what they have planned?
It is not realistic.
Peter.
-We should already imagine what we will find on Empycrist. We are not certain
that
we will be able to live on it.
John.
-We know for sure that there is enough
oxygen and water. So, life is possible.
Paul.
-Life is possible, but does it mean that the plants will provide the food we need?
Will we be poisoned? Will we find fishes and animals
we will be able to eat?
Peter.
-We are not obliged to eat meat;
vegetables will do the trick.
Jenny.
-We could multiply Barbara's apes...
Barbara.
-Are you...
Jenny.
-I am joking Barbara. I am certain that Peter will find a suitable substitute
Made of vegetable proteins.
Barbara.
-Are there oceans and rivers on Empycrist II.
Peter.
-Yes, there are. Moreover, the temperatures, I mean the climates, seem to
resemble ours. That's why we are almost certain that we will find a natural
environment that will suit us.
Jenny.
-Do you really think that we will find a
superior life form?
Peter.

-I hope so... However... we might be compelled to schedule their own death if we implement Port Isabel's plan.

John.

-In that case, I assure you that we will not implement it. I don't want to repeat American history. No nation can afford to build itself from a manslaughter. Murder cannot be the foundation stone of a nation. Romulus cannot kill Remus, or else you compel people to envisage barbarity and plan the downfall of your country. The Greeks and the Romans disappeared because of their primordial vices. I promise that this will not happen again. I will be proud to be the dangerous plotter who will create a new society based on virtue, not crime. The meeting is closed.

PETER IS IN THE GREENHOUSE: he wants to think about the mission. Everything is so artificial there, but his own garden on Earth was already a man-made realisation. I don't know why gardeners persist in aligning what they grow. Sometimes, I believe they would also like to align weeds in order to pull them out easily. I am aware of the productivity logic of the farmers who improve the yield of the crops that way and allow their dreadful machines to steal the work of a great many people, crush their hopes and ruin their lives. I don't really understand why they line up daffodils, tulips, or rose bushes in their ornamental gardens. It is not really pretty. I would even say that it is quite sad, for it reminds me of idiosyncrasies shared by many people: aren't human beings straight lines that will never meet? I might be slightly pessimistic, but, even when people live together (some of them are even married), they are still parallel lines. They pretend to live together; however, there are no real mental interactions between them. They remain lonely their whole lives. There is nothing worse than this crowded loneliness.

Peter's greenhouse is much more impressive than his garden, and I know why: there is less symmetry there! It is not a French formal garden; it rather looks like an English garden. No, it is an oasis in the very middle of these interstellar solitudes. It is insane: all the climates have been recreated and the most tropical species almost touch plants you could find on the top of the mountains or in very cold places. For instance, he has placed a bilberry bush next to a mango tree, and they both grow very well! The result is... improbable.

Peter is seated on the moss, in front of the marble fountain. The sound of pouring water seems to help him think. What is he thinking? The scent of the orange blossom is heady. Is it April yet? No, it is January. Time is meaningless! The orange trees have all decided to bloom at the same time because they want to fructify. Peter thinks that it will be easy to plant all the plants on Empycrist. He will find a suitable location and help them a bit so that they may stand the climate. The main problem is pollination because, although they are all self-fertile, they need the assistance of insects, especially honey bees. He has a colony here. These small creatures are really helpful. Regardless of the hour or the day they work! Thanks to them, the fragrant blossoms of the citrus trees will soon turn into tiny little fruits. On Empycrist, since the planet is huge, he will have to find a solution to keep them together, for they are not faithful and like to gather all types of pollen from many different flowers. He might have to limit the growth of the native plants. Please Peter, don't make the same mistakes... don't destroy everything; let nature act, for she might be more intelligent than you! Besides, you could have a nice surprise: nature could even feed you on Empycrist II.

Chapter 3:
The gaze of the monkey.

Barbara's laboratory is very quiet today. The apes are sleeping. The night light, with its blue reflections, is painting shivering shadows that will soon wake up, shout and even try to speak. The five chimpanzees are still sleeping, but Adam, Dr. Frankenstein's little protégé, is stretching his limbs. The cages are so small! How can they stand that? They are not mistreated; nevertheless, those big animals do not live a normal, pleasant life. Is plenty of food every day worth the pain? Freedom is not only a human claim, it is also an animal necessity. Wild animals have a function in the universe and they must act freely, according to their animal nature, in order to fulfil what nature has ordered. Don't put them in cages, or else their nature will alter. Don't imprison them, for they are not guilty. It is so pleasant to see a bird fly in the morning breeze and so sad to see it bite the bars of its prison.

Barbara.
-Wake up, Adam.

Adam.
-Rrrr...
Barbara.
-We have a lot of work today. We are going to learn some new words; we are going to try to pronounce them well and, maybe, we are going to write, aren't we?
Adam.
-Rrrr...
Barbara to herself while making a cup of coffee.

-They bear a very close resemblance to us. We almost share the same genetic material. They are our first cousins, and their brains are not that small: 410 grams is the weight of a human child's brain! I can teach them how to speak. I am sure that they think. So, they can speak, even if their larynxes are not as effectual as ours. They seem so human. They are more intelligent than dogs!

Adam.

-Rrrr...

Barbara.

-What are you saying, Adam?

Adam.

-Rrrr...

Barbara.

-You are so intelligent. 410 grams: it is not a lot, but I will teach you how to become... human. Let's start with the name of fruits: banana!

Repeat after me: BANANA.

Adam.

-Hiii, hiii, hiii.

Barbara.

-Not bad; the diction is not impeccable, but we almost understand what you are saying. Well, let's use another word: pineapple.

Adam, say PINEAPPLE.

Adam.

-Hiii... hiii, hiii.

Barbara.

-The rhythm is good... I know you understand me. Just say APPLE.

Adam.

-Hiii, hiii.

Barbara.

-Good, good boy, Adam.

Take this pen and draw it now.

THE MONKEY TAKES THE pen and draws what is neither a pineapple nor an apple. Nevertheless, there is something on the piece of paper. Does he understand her after all?

Barbara.

-It is beautiful, and so realistic! You are an artist, Adam... more gifted than Rimisky. You are as talented as the Magdalenian hominids in their caves: they left the outline of their hands, some impressive paintings of animals, and you are doing the same. Please, draw me a sheep... No, it is too difficult; draw me a chicken.
Adam.
-Rrrr... rrrr....
Barbara.
-Let me see... Well, I don't understand... It does not look like a chicken. Pronounce CHICKEN.
Adam.
-Hiii, hiii.
Barbara.
-No, it's not that. I should teach you first to pronounce "chicken", then you would be able to draw what you can name and therefore understand. Well, let's try something else. We are going to walk. Just imitate me. Walk, slide... head up... elegance... grace... humanity...
Adam jumping and happy to be outside his cage.
-Haaa, haaa, haaa.
Barbara.
-No, it's not that. You are aping me! Stand up and walk... Do not put your hands on the floor. Raise your hands... Slide... You are not really elegant. Nature has not been kind to you. Man has received more than you. You are quite ugly, Adam. Don't jump! Don't be a bad boy;
behave yourself,
and stop talking! You, little brain!

Jenny.
-Am I interrupting anything important?
Barbara.
-Not really. Adam is a naughty boy:
he does not want to work today.
Jenny.

-Barbara, it is an ape, not a human: it usually eats black plums or African pears, and it neither writes philosophy essays, nor laugh when the other inmates make fun of themselves.

Barbara.

-They do laugh.

Jenny.

-No, they don't: they just shout! Laughter is a human privilege. Man is the only creature that laughs. Laughter is the path to the discovery of difference between man's behavior and reality. It compels him to perceive madness and flee it. As a matter of fact, you laugh at yourself or someone like you; you don't laugh at others. If you do so, you just express wild hatred, which aims to destroy all the others. The smile you see on their faces is a rictus, the devilish grimace given by madness.

Your monkeys don't smile; they grimace.

Barbara.

-These monkeys are not what you want to see in them: they are neither the apostles of Satan nor the reflection of your hatred of... mankind. They are rather like children, very young children. They have a little brain: 410 grams. If their skulls had been larger, their brains would have been able to grow... I should try surgery... do something with their skulls. The first hominids were really like them: small brains in small skulls. Something happened, and the skull of the monkeys grew; then the brain of the hominids reached the fantastic weight of one thousand grams, and then **one thousand AND four hundred grrramzzzzzz**... Mankind was born that way: **something** enabled man's skull to grow. I want to find this **something**.

Jenny.

-Man is not an animal, and you won't turn Adam into a human being. Man's ancestors were not monkeys but humans: human nature comes from human nature and simian nature from simian nature. The parietal painters looked like their hominid ancestors who skillfully made knives out of stones: they had a human soul. You infer the nature of something from flesh and bones. It does not work like that, for the essence of everything comes from something matter cannot explain.

Barbara.

-Humans are animals: mammals without fur! We share the same feelings; we are the same!

Jenny.

-We are not, since your nature is unique. Man is the only creature that does not reach its own nature automatically. Your ape is an ape by nature: it knows what to do and how to behave and live in perfect harmony with the rest of the Creation if you don't alter its nature! Man never reaches his nature without the combination of some factors. Of course, nature stubbornly compels him to pass through different stages that enable the child to become an adult as they allow him to acknowledge barbarity and wisdom,
but it is he who consciously chooses to be a humane human or not. You are so... you are so... Darwinian!

Barbara.

-Matter explains a lot of things. The body of the animals at least explains why the fittest survive
and the weakest perish.

Jenny.

-The strongest do not survive: look at the dinosaurs.

Barbara.

-Your argument is specious, Jenny.

Jenny.

-Well... maybe. Man is not that strong...

Barbara.

-His brain is!

Jenny.

-I know, look at the Capnodis Tenebrionis, this poor little thing.

Barbara.

-It is not what I call a poor little thing. It is a robust organism that is highly adaptable to change
since it normally eats the peduncle of the leaves of the apricot tree but can change diets when this food is not available. I have seen some, in the South of Spain, that ate the avocado trees' leathery leaves! It is a very good example of the domination of the fittest.

Jenny.

- It's quite the opposite! This beetle is not relevant, but its food is meaningful. It always attacks the strongest trees, which means
that the weakest ones survive! So?
Barbara.
-Darwin was not a plant biologist!
Jenny.
-Spit it out; the facts don't fit the theory!
Barbara.
-By the way, what are you doing here?
Jenny.
-... I don't remember!

Barbara.
-Let's continue, Adam. Take your building blocks. No! We are going to do something new now. I am going to teach you the American Sign Language.
Adam.
-Rrrr...
Barbara.
-What? Is there anything wrong?
Adam.
-Rrrr... rrrr....
Barbara.
-I prefer that. How stubborn you can be sometimes! Show me your hands... They are beautiful... so strong... Show me your arms... Move them a little bit, not too much... You are not flexible. You are not elegant... You are an ape!... It is not your fault, it's mine... I should have studied bigger brains. Do you know that gorillas' brains weigh 500 grams? It is a great quantity of grey matter! My colleagues, at the University of Edelpic, have tried to make them speak. They have failed. It is strange, yours is smaller but you seem quite smart... Anyway, I should have studied the dolphins: 1700 grams of pure intelligence! Their larynxes and their mouths cannot produce the sounds I need...
Flesh is everything... isn't it?
Adam.

-....
Barbara.
-You are not saying anything.
Adam.

-....
Barbara.
-You could say something.
Adam.

-....
Barbara.
-After all I have done for you. You are so... ungrateful. Do not forget that I am the one who turned your obtuse intelligence into what you are today. I have created you!
What do you think of that?
Adam.

-....
Barbara.
-Speak!

WHAT A STRANGE COUPLE: the talkative blond Dr. Frankenstein and the silent brown-eyed chimpanzee. There are too many Dr. Frankensteins in universities and too many enslaved apes. The former are not smart enough to realize that their researches are pointless, whereas the existence of the latter cannot increase the level of awareness of these stupid doctors. With its big black eyes, it is looking at the wild baby-blue eyes of Barbara. Both are salt statues gazing at the bottomless emptiness of the other. What do you want to tell her, Adam? I am not her; you can answer me! Adam... can you think?...

Chapter 4:
It cannot be the end.

The computer that controls the Invictus is a work of art. The engineers who designed it wanted to create a machine that would be able to think instead of the crew. Man is not always driven by rational thoughts: a reliable apparatus can give him accurate information, but, for mysterious reasons, he will not understand the unquestionable facts, which will lead him to make a wrong decision and, sometimes, crash a plane or a spaceship. The mission was too important to run such a risk. We must not underestimate the stress generated by these long missions or the mental health consequences. One year in a tin can drives rats, monkeys and human beings crazy! Hence, the computer scientists put their heart into the making of this artificial intelligence. However, I know that it does not think! Actually, it combines pieces of information and tries to generate a logical conclusion, but it only deals with technical things: vectors, algorithms, and square roots of highly foreseeable numbers. If you feed information on life and human feelings into it, you will always bring disaster. There is no such thing as artificial intelligence, for computers are the slaves to other people's will. There is no intelligence where slavery reigns. It is something that comes from the acceptance of one's own bottomless ignorance. It does not follow the logic of the omnipotence of other people's belief in the grandeur of technology. The awareness of one's own limitations is the key to the holy garden of reason. Besides, I don't like its voice and manners. It behaves as if it were a human being, but it only apes its creators: parrots also speak, but they don't pretend that they are more than birds.

Computer.
-John, may I have a word with you?
John.
-You may.

Computer.
-According to the data, we may get into trouble when we reach the vicinity of Militus.
John.
-What kind of trouble?
Computer.
-Meteorites.
John.
-Don't we have an efficient deflector shield against that?
Computer.
-Yes, we have, of course.
John.
-Did you turn it on?
Computer.
-Yes, we did.
John.
-So, what's the problem?
Computer.
-We might make a miscalculation.
John.
-A miscalculation! Can you make one, computer?
Computer.
-Of course not! I am perfect.
John.
-I hope so. When do we reach Militus?
Computer.
-In ten minutes.
John.
-Already!
Computer.
-Yes, John... May I say anything else?
John.
-You may.
Computer.

-We have just been hit by small debris,
but there is no damage…
John.
-Is the deflector shield at full power?
Computer.
-No, the information I have says that the danger zone will be reached in five
minutes.
John.
-Raise the level of protection right now.
Computer.
-It is not necessary.
John.
-Raise it.
Computer.
-We have been hit by a meteorite. There is some damage. Deflector shield: full
power.
John.
-Describe the damage.
Computer.
-There are holes in the structure. There is at least one in the water tank. Level of
water supply:
3.12 %! There is one hole in the shuttle garage. The shuttles are OK. There is an
unidentified problem in the power plant. Nuclear reactor
shut down… the emergency power generator
is operating.
John.
-Do we have enough power
to continue the journey?
Computer.
-No.
John.
-How much power do we have?
Computer.
-12% of your needs.

John.
-Can we return to Earth?
Computer.
-... I don't know.
John.
-Is it a joke?
Computer.
-No.
John.
-Why don't you know?
Computer.
-... Because there are random factors.
John.
-Explain yourself.
Computer.
-We may hit another meteorite on our way back.
John.
-Why?
Computer.
-Why not?
John.
-Your hypothesis must be corroborated by facts.
Computer.
-... John, may I...
John.
-Shut up, computer!

I GUESS THAT JOHN IS upset. He has turned off the computer's voice. The infallibility of things is an illusion. Ideas are sometimes infallible, not things. Well, I only know one: the poetical movement of heavenly geometry.

Paul.
-I have felt a small vibration, John.

Barbara.
-The power has gone off in my laboratory.
Jenny.
-There is no running water in my cabin.
Peter.
- John, I don't understand: the heater, in the greenhouse, has stopped blowing warm air.
John.
-We have been hit by a meteorite.
We are having problems with...
Barbara.
-How is it possible? Don't we have
a deflector shield?
John.
-The computer made a fatal miscalculation.
Paul.
-It is impossible: computers do not miscalculate, they just misinterpret facts.
Jenny.
-You mean that they misjudge them.
Peter.
-I would rather say that
they misunderstand them.
John.
-**It messed up everything**!
Paul, Jenny, Peter and Barbara.
-Oh!
Paul.
-So, what are we supposed to do?
John.
-Fix the problem without
the help of this stupid machine.
Barbara.
-Beware, John, he can hear you: he might be offended. Have you noticed? He is not talking.
John.

-**It** is a thing; **it** cannot be offended,
and I have disabled the speakers.
Paul.
-Is there much damage?
John.
-We have lost a lot of water and the power plant is not functioning. I don't really know what is wrong inside, but if we don't find it, we are not certain that we will be able to continue the journey. Water is not a real problem,
since we are next to Militus.
Paul.
-Do we have enough power to go back?
John.
-I don't know.
Barbara.
-Are we going to die?
John.
-It is not impossible.
Paul.
-We cannot die. If we die, mankind will disappear. They won't be able to survive for long.
Peter.
- Humanity cannot end in that way.
Paul.
-It is not humanity that will end but barbarity. Actually, the history of mankind has not started yet. What you read in books is a
boring description of killings.
Peter.
-It is even worse.
Paul.
-Why?
Peter.

-Because dawn does not sound the trumpet of the Apocalypse. It is a beginning, the moment when the feeble light of the sun illumines the roads which myriads of conscious minds will have to follow in order to build a graceful future

together. The beginning has not started! It cannot be the end. I must go to the
power plant.
Paul.
-I will go with you.
Jenny, Barbara, John.
-So will I.

THE POWER PLANT IS located at the bottom of the spacecraft. At the end of
an endless corridor, the heavy security door displays a radiation warning sign that
makes them feel uncomfortable. Do they really want to forget that the fantastic
quantity of electricity they need comes from this source of energy? They open
the door. In the airlock, they put on their personal protective equipment and
their helmets. A soft blue light wraps them in an unreal iridescent outfit. Their
breathing accelerates. Their angst is palpable. John faces the control panel in
search of the causes of the breakdown. The others snoop around this place in
order to check whether there is a mechanical problem. It is strange: there are
neither holes in the walls nor deformations.
Paul.
-I don't see anything.
Jenny.
-Neither do I.
Peter.
-Everything is OK here.
Barbara.
-John, I am scared!
John.
-What's wrong Barbara? What did you see?
Barbara.
-... I must see my husband!
Peter.
-John, she did not see anything.
Jenny walking towards her.
-Barbara, there is no reason to panic: you are not alone. We are next to you.

Barbara.
-Our wedding was so beautiful. I remember my dress... I resembled a princess, a princess without a crown but with an exquisite rhinestone tiara... Jenny, do you miss your husband?
Jenny.
-... I would like to say yes...
Paul.
-I miss my wife!
Barbara.
-We are alone here... I have chosen my husband;
I have not chosen to be with you.
Paul.
-You never choose all the people with whom you are, but you always choose to build a present together and a brighter future.
Barbara.
-... Maybe. The same kind of people
must build their future together.
Paul.
-Not the same people; different... I should say very dissimilar people must determine in which direction they want to go. Sameness leads to nowhere since it prevents the possibility of choosing, along with any kind of movement. Sameness is the negation of life and, at the same time, the embodiment of the fear of life.
Barbara.
-How could very different people
choose the same path?
Paul.
-Because, in spite of their different opinions, they share one essential quality: goodness. Goodness has different faces but one essence. Once established, it would guarantee its propagation and would eternally remain the owner of a humanized universe.
Barbara, Jenny and Peter.
-...
John.
-I think I have found what is going wrong.

Peter.
-Evilness is the owner of our world!
John.
-... The computer has switched off the power plant without rhyme or reason!... Barbara, I think that you will see your husband again! Jenny, check whether there is a leak in the cooling system.
Jenny.
-There is nothing, John...
John.
-Let's turn the power on.
Paul.
-Wow... light again.
Jenny.
-You are luminous, John.
Peter.
-You mean brilliant!
Barbara.
-I would rather say bright!
John.
-No, I am not; Paul is!

Chapter 5:
Water.

Militus is a yellowish planet, a kind of gigantic Sahara desert, a dusty mineral reality. It is not appealing unless you like geology. Actually, there are lots of strange stony structures once carved by water. The hills look like immobile giants waiting for an improbable David. The wind carries sand in its infuriated arms. Sometimes, it sprinkles this powdery silicon on the canyons and the missing oceans. It is a scintillating snowfall that covers our giants with suffocating dust. Where has the water gone? Geomorphology does not lie: it is water that has created these shapes, not the wind. Is it below the surface? Yes, but where exactly? There is no time to waste: they need water and must find some. The wordless computer has given them a map which shows the sites where they could find the precious liquid. Will it be fresh water? It is very unlikely, but salt water will be easily turned into drinking water in the Invictus. As for the pleasure of diving into the tempestuous turquoise mountain streams, they can just forget it, but it is not important, since they will soon reach Empycrist II. There, they will rediscover the infancy of planet Earth. They will enjoy the wonders of what they lost and will regain.

John.
-Paul, what is your opinion about the maps?
Paul.
-They are pretty, for there are lots of beautiful colors, but I am not convinced that there is water on this planet. There is no trace of plant life. Everything is so dry!
John.
-Militus is not Mars: there is an atmosphere, which proves that water has not escaped into space.
Paul.

-Where are we going to land?

John.

-In the canyon you see over there.

Paul.

-Beware, it is a riverbed.

John.

-Paul, there is no water
on the surface of this planet.

Paul.

-... Of course... How will we be able to find a spot where there is ground water?

John.

-Elementary, Paul: find limestone and
you will also find water underneath.

Paul.

-Do you think that we will see
traces of moisture on the ground?

John.

-Don't worry; your detector will help you! I know you are a physicist, not a
geologist.

Paul.

-John, I think I don't like stones. Everything is so mineral on this planet. Even a
fennec would ask for shade, flowers and water. I hate deserts; it is not only the
heat that I don't like,
it is also this unbearable silence.

John.

-I have visited the Sahara Desert... in summer. I remember... the sky: so blue!
Azure, like my grandmother's eyes. A beautiful colour for a woman's eyes... a
bewitching colour.

Paul.

-The bluest blue needs grey. I visited Scotland in August 3057. I remember the
tormented clouds, the sound of the raindrops on the roofs at night, the scent of

the air in the morning, and the greyish lakes that are never thirsty. I love the rain.

John.
-We are going to land.
Paul.
-We must find a lake, in a cave.
John.
-I am not very optimistic, Paul.

John.
-Does your localizer work?
Paul.
-Yes, it does. So does my radio.
John.
-It's best to separate in order to cover a lot of ground. Go this way; I am going that way. Never switch off your radio.
Paul.
-I won't.

•••

Paul.
-I have been walking for an hour and
I haven't seen any trace of moisture.
John.
-What is the nature of the soil?
Paul.
-It is limestone. I can see the sediment layers on the sides of the canyon. It is
such a long history. It is hard to believe there was a river here, before.
What happened to this planet?
John.
-Its orbit changed, which modified the composition of its atmosphere. It was so
close to its sun that a portion of the water evaporated. I guess that the other
portion
is underneath the ground.
Paul.
-John, where you are? Do you see these
strange hills that look like giants?
John.
-Yes, I do, and I feel like a Lilliputian. It is strange: I don't see you on my
detector. Is it working?
Paul.
-It does not seem to be working, but it is not a problem: since I am following
the riverbed,
I can't get lost.
John.
-There is a lot of wind here, and so much sand.
Paul.

-I am covered with dust. What an unpleasant place. The Earth is not like that.

John.

-Oh, no, it was not like that.

Paul.

-What's this noise?

John.

-Some stones are falling.

Paul.

-It is an earthquake! I...

John.

-Could you say that again?

Paul.

-...

John.

-Paul, do you copy?

Paul.

-...

John.

-**PAUL**, are you OK?

Paul.

-Yes, John; I am just thinking...
How did we get here?

John.

-I don't know.

Paul.

-You don't know or you don't want to know!

John.

-I don't want to know it.

Paul.

-But, if you don't, and if we don't, we will never learn from our mistakes. We
force our species to disappear. John, I am asking you again!

John.

-Because... they are insane! They are unable to realize that they are not God!

Paul.

-They are not insane: insane people know that they are not God. Actually, they believe that He is about to break them into pieces, which is incorrect and proves that they are mad!

John.

-Because... they are simpleminded.

Paul.

-Have you noticed? They seem so normal but, at the same time, intellectually handicapped and desperately... childish. Most of them are five-year-old boys and girls sharing the same
daydreams, selfishness and whims.

John.

-Maturity is the aim of a human's life.

Paul.

-No, it is the beginning.

John.

-What is the aim in that case, and what is the purpose of the universe?

Paul.

-You know the answer! Man is the ultimate goal: you may not understand it, but you do perceive it!

John.

-I have found water; I can smell it.

Paul.

-I am coming, John.

Paul.

-Where is it?

John.

-In that direction. Look here, there is some water, not a lot, but it seems that there is a stream, which means that we could find some more.

Paul.

-You are right: there is a stream.

Let's follow this tunnel.

John.

-There is a strange smell.

Paul.

-Yes, it smells like mildew or... fungus!

John.

-But my detector says there is no life here!

Paul.

-The eternal life of fungi is not considered life
by your detector!

John.

-Look at the drips on the walls.

Paul.

-Don't walk that fast; I can hardly breathe.

John.

-Hurry up, I am sure that I am going to find water. Look over there: a pool.

Paul.

-Did you hear that?

John.

-What?

Paul.

-Drops. Keep quiet!... Yes, drops.

John.

-Of course, the sound of water drops falling in a...

THEY SUDDENLY ENTERED a huge cave where they found... a lake. Paul looked at the water as if it were the Holy Grail. He touched it with his right hand and put it feverishly on his right cheek: the salt almost burned his skin! John kneeled down and touched it. The light of his torch turned the opaque salty lake into a transparent aquamarine. Then they slowly stood up and went back to the shuttle in order to bring back a pipe. They put the end of the pipe in the very middle of the lake and sat down. It started to suck up the liquid. They remained silent. The noise of the pump drowned out the sound of the water drops. They looked like two grateful believers, in a deserted cathedral, thanking God for this extraordinary gift. There were no prayers, no songs, no demented organs, and no inspired sermons, just faith and eternity. Sometimes words are meaningless.

Thoughts are truer than words; they are cathedrals palpitating in the thirstiest deserts. Man does not need to speak; he must feel, understand and act. He is his own cathedral.

37

Chapter 6:
Bad news from the Earth.

Dizziness! A child is born; he grows up in inhumanity and remains all his life in barbarity, but he begets a child. Dizziness! His daughter takes the same path and gives birth to the grandchild of the first monster. The history of mankind is but an everlasting inferno, for man has decided to eat his own liver forever. I am falling: the idea of an endless tragedy is sheer torture.

They got the news this morning, and it is not good. The Statue of Liberty has decided to burn its bronze toga! The Creator cannot destroy His creature because it does not belong to him anymore. He has blessed it with the possibility of consciousness. Hence, it belongs to the logic of the One who creates things and inspires people. Individual consciousness prevents man from disappearing. What happens if he does not reach this stage? He turns gold into lead. This morning the sun woke up a world of lead; the Statue of Liberty opened its mouth in order to pronounce the unspeakable word: WAR!

Can you hear this sound? They are blowing the trumpets, for they want to destroy Masada. They have donned their shining suits of armor in order to hide their vices. On the crowns of their leaders there are scintillating rubies that will soon be stained with the blood they do not want to see. Eve of the battle: the quixotic murderers murmur, the walls of Masada shiver, I am in pain. In the middle of a glade, a drummer boy awakens the beasts. Is it Dresden or Gettysburg? All battles are alike. Sinners, please, don't do this! You cannot be that bad. Don't you know that red is the colour of sorrow? Sinners, do you really think you are going to become gods? Destruction is not a celestial attribute but a chthonic subterfuge. Fools, you are about to become the conscious embodiment of evil. Please, say no to yourselves!

Can you hear this noise? Is it the roar of the drums? No, it is the sound of the heartbeats of the crucifiers and their victims, it is the echo of the bombs falling on

Dresden, Tokyo and me. Planet Earth is burning: the skies are wrathful. It's noon. Vapors of savagery are infecting the air: they can hardly breathe, but they can kill. The Trevi Fountain is crying: the past of Rome is shaking. The giant sequoias of California are burning: the present of mankind is running away. Hell! Hell on Earth! The Hermes of Praxiteles won't be able to protect the little Dionysus he is holding in his arms. It is a sad sunny day, and the statues, in the archeological museum of Delphi, are bleeding. Apollo is in mourning: the center of the world is hiccupping. Perched on the top of the Tholos, a falcon is gazing at the world. On one side there is mankind and its unbearable cruelty; on the other side there is nature and its peaceful beauty. It cannot look at the first without thinking about the other. Its head turns in the direction of the sea. Time stops. In front of it, there is a sea of olive trees and an ocean of orange trees. Green, everything is so green. It breathes and jumps in the lightness of the breeze. The sun carries it to the empyreal blue of the sky. Blue, I want you to be blue: blue the Gulf of Corinth, blue the skies over Delphi, blue the eyes of the silent charioteer in the sanctuary. You cannot kill the bird: it does belong to the eternal nature. You cannot kill the falcon: I am sure that it will escape. White falcon, fly high, higher than their inhumane nature.

Test director.
-John, can you hear me?
John.
-Yes, I can.
Test director.
-How are you?
John.
-I miss the Earth, especially the daily cycle.
Test director.
-And the others?
John.
-They are fine. There is so much space here that we barely see one another. Each one of us is lost
in his own solitude.

Test director.
-So, they won't hear me.
John.
-Oh no, I haven't seen them in two days
and I can assure you that I am alone.
Test director.
-Did you watch the news?
John.
-I haven't, for it is always the same thing: a terrorist attack here, a revolution
there, and a war over there. There is nothing new under the sun: four Romans
and five Carthaginians
are lying on the ground!
Test director.
-You should have watched the news.
John.
-What's the matter?
Test director.
-There is a war going on here.
John.
-You mean the United States are involved in a conflict somewhere in the world!
Test director.
-I mean there is a full-scale war.
John.
-Are there many Romans and Carthaginians
who are involved?
Test director.
-The whole planet. It is World War III here!
John.
-Are you joking?
Test director.
-I am not, and that's why I want to talk to you.
John.
-I guess that you want me to go faster, but, you see, if there are no plants on
Empycrist II, we will not be able to feed the people you are planning
to send there.

Test director.
-You are missing the point.
We must cancel the mission.
John.
-You may give up on the stupid idea of mass migration, but I can assure you
that I am going to Empycrist.
Test director.
-I am asking you to come back.
John.
-You must be joking. If there is a war, Earth is not a safe! So, why should we
come back? To be immolated on the altar of your insanity?
Test director.
-You must come back.
John.
-I won't: why should I obey you?
Test director.
-We pay; you obey!
John.
-In your wild world, money does not mean anything anymore. So, I don't care.
Test director.
-We have the power...
John.
-Which power? What does it mean? You have the power to kill yourself: that's
it. You don't have the power to give the orders. Reason commands, not madness.
Answer me: are you sane?
Test director.
-... Ye...
John.
-You are not! You are mad... all of you!
Test director.
-... We are your employer!
John.
-Not any more: I quit!
Test director.
-You cannot do that. This has never

HAPPENED BEFORE... and why would you do that?

John.
-Because my reason compels me to obey
my volition, not your ravings.
Test director.
-But...
John.
-Shut up! The conversation is over.

John.
-Jenny, the flight director upsets.
Jenny.
-Why?
John.
-He wants us to come back.
Jenny.
-Why should we come back? Have these
people changed their minds
about the mass migration?
John.
-Well, yes... Have you watched the news?
Jenny.
-Of course not... Planet Earth is so far
away already... I think that's the least
of my worries.
John.
-They are in a predicament.
Jenny.
-This is not a surprise.
John.
-It is worse this time.

JOURNEY TO EMPYCRIST II

Jenny.
-Worse than what? Worse than Spartacus' ordeal on the Appian Way? Worse than World War II? How can it be worse? It can't! Don't you remember? History books are still bleeding!

John.
-It is worse because I think that they have already destroyed a huge part of mankind and... nobody told me, but... I think they have used nuclear weapons. You can easily imagine
the consequences.

Jenny.
-They don't need atomic bombs to kill themselves. Give them a knife and they will kill all the people in their neighborhood. Don't give them anything and they will strangle their brothers and sisters. Even if their hands were tied together, they could nuke the whole universe in their minds. John, what do you really know about this war?

John.
-I don't know a lot of things; I am just guessing.

Jenny.
-I prefer facts because, if I start guessing, I will imagine the worst-case scenario. I will remember that man doesn't always bury the dead. I will realize that he fled from the charming painted caves of Lascaux in order to burn
in this hellish present.

John.
-Decadence was not the only option... Call them!

Jenny.
-Port Isabel, Jenny's speaking. Can you hear me?

Test director.
-...

Jenny.
-Is there a connection problem?

John.
-No, everything works fine.

Jenny.
-Can you hear me?

Test director.

-...
John.
-If you want information, I can show you the records the computer has received.
I guess you will get to know what has been bombed.
Jenny.
-I need something more accurate. They work for the U. S. Army: every day they
receive the military reports.
John.
-Port Isabel, do you copy?
Test director.

-...
John.
-Well, we have lost contact with them.
Jenny.
-We are alone now.
John.
-We have always been alone! We are just without them but with ourselves!
Jenny.
-I am scared!
John.
-Oh please, Jenny, you are beginning
to look like Barbara!
Jenny.
-What are we going to do?
John.
-Go to Empycrist: there is no other option.
I have decided to go there!
Jenny.
-You can decide for yourself, not for the others.
Our lives are also at stake.
Jenny to herself.
-What am I going to do?
John.
-Get some rest; we will decide tomorrow.

Chapter 7:
What must we do?

John.

-Thank you for being here on such short notice. Jenny has told you that we have lost contact with Port Isabel and that there is a war on Planet Earth. So, we need to talk about what we are going to do. Actually, there are two possibilities: reach Empycrist II, settle down and live, or go back to Earth, get killed, or starve, or whatever!

Barbara.

-You are not really objective, John.

Paul.

-John is right: if we go back, we won't survive.

Barbara.

-This is your point of view, not mine.

Jenny.

-It is not a point of view; it is the truth.

Barbara.

-Truth does not exist, there are only opinions.

Paul.

-The universe is not an opinion; it is a fact.

Jenny.

-Or a cumbersome opinion!

Barbara.

-I mean...

Paul.

-Poor Barbara, you don't mean anything! There is no meaning in your life but illusions!

Barbara.

45

-I want to see my husband...
Paul.
-He is dead!
Peter.
-Paul, you could be more tactful.
John.
-Anyway... we must vote.
Jenny.
-We? Could you define "we"?
John.
-I mean the five of us.
Jenny.
-You mean the four of us.
John speaking to Jenny.
-What's the matter with you?
Jenny.
-What's the matter with Barbara! We cannot recognize the validity of an election
if the voters are not perfectly sane.
Paul.
-It is not enough. They should also be intelligent and wise. So I am not certain that there are four voters here... I would say: three!
Jenny.
-What are you hinting at?
Paul.
-You are not what some people call a genius! You spend much time learning languages, but what do you do with all that knowledge? Nothing! You can say "hello" and "could you pass me the salt, please" in 27 different languages, but we never hear you say intelligent things, especially in English! I assume that you only speak
words of wisdom in Coptic!

Jenny.

-At least I speak; I am not dumb like Peter.

Peter.

-I am not dumb: I have nothing to say to you. You are neither pretty nor intelligent. You are so unpleasant and ordinary.

Jenny.

-...

Paul.

-Well, we are not here to love one another.

We must vote; that's it.

Jenny.

-I don't want Barbara to vote.

Peter.

-I don't want Jenny to vote.

John.

-I know; we won't vote: I will decide. Democracy is a dangerous regime; it always leads to dictatorship, massacres and so on.

Paul.

-You are right, John, and as a smart guy, or rather, a smart captain, you would make a good dictator. I've got a better idea: we should be evaluated on our mental capabilities. Tests do not lie, even though some of them are questionable.

Peter.

-That's the understatement of the year! A schizophrenic can possess an IQ of 125, which is higher than that of a well-balanced person!

Paul.

-The IQ test is, of course, not reliable. I dare say it is always illogical. Hermann Goring, a smart guy with an intelligence quotient of 138, is responsible for the death of almost 60 million people. This is not what I call a sign of intelligence! But don't worry: I have other tests dealing with interpersonal skills and general knowledge. I can assure you that

they give a good idea of the

level of intelligence of people.

John.

-Well, let's try your tests.

Jenny.

-I don't want to take these tests.

John.
-Barbara will be evaluated and you don't want to follow this procedure?
Jenny.
-The problem is not me but her!
John.
-You will follow the rules, my rules. Tomorrow, like all of us, you will take the
test.
Jenny, the conversation is over!

John.
-I got the results, and they make sense. Paul achieved the best results: 97% of the
answers are right. It is not a surprise. Paul is very clever and knowledgeable; isn't
he? Peter scored 90%; I scored 87%. As for Jenny, 48 % of the answers are...
wrong, which is a lot.
Barbara.
-Did I get a good grade?
John.
-You scored 51%.
Barbara.
-I don't understand: the questions were so easy.
John.
-Apparently not: you had a problem
with the interpersonal items!
Barbara.
-What does it mean?
John.
-It means that your perception of others is almost psychotic. It is clear that you
do not understand people's elementary behavior.
Paul.
-Give her an example so that
she may understand more easily.
John.

-You are right, Paul. Well, let's take item 37: "what do you fell when someone you don't know looks at you in the street"? You answered without hesitation: "I feel important: when men look at me, it's because I am pretty. Men always fall in love with me at first sight".

Paul.

-A very interesting item.

Peter.

-A very interesting answer too.

Barbara.

-It is true: men adore me!

John.

-The problem is that a person is not a man; a person is a person! It could have been a woman.

Jenny.

-It could have been a monkey!

John.

-Stop making fun of people, Jenny: your results do not allow such behavior! So, Barbara, what is your reaction when a woman looks at you
in the street?

Barbara.

-I hate that. It is always for the same reason: jealousy. Women are mean: they believe that I am going to steal their husbands because I am prettier than they! Look at Jenny; she is rude to me because she is jealous. But it's insane! I am not going to steal your husband: he is on Planet Earth, not here!
You should see a psychiatrist!

Paul.

-It is not completely wrong.

John.

-No, it is not completely wrong, but it is completely stupid. Barbara, you won't vote.

Barbara.

-I...

John.

-Barbara, don't make me lose my temper.

Barbara sighing.

-I won't, John...
Jenny.
-Fine, the four of us will vote.
John.
-No!
Jenny.
-No?
John.
-You won't vote!
Jenny.
-Why?
John.
-The interpersonal skills items are OK, even though they show your true personality.
Peter.
-She is so unpleasant.
Paul.
-And ill-mannered. The kind of person you don't introduce to your mother!
Peter.
-The kind of person you are happy not to know!
John.
-Actually, this test reveals your abysmal lack of general knowledge, and this is a problem. Sane people can decide for themselves and others thanks to knowledge. They are sane, which enables them to perceive what is real or not; that's fine! However, without knowledge, they cannot fully understand the consequences of their deeds and are also condemned to ignore the essence of everything.
Peter.
-Give us an example of her lack of education.
John.
-Item 79: "who wrote Romeo and Juliet"? Your appalling answer is ◇ drum roll please ◇
...: "Tchaikovsky"!
Peter and Paul.
-Gosh!

John.
-Isn't it a crime against humanity?
Peter.
-Too many ballet classes maybe!
John.
-It gets worse; listen to that: "who sculpted the Hermes of Praxiteles"? Her
answer: "Phidias"!
Barbara.
-She must be crazy.
John.
-You might be right, Barbara. Jenny,
you won't vote!
Jenny.
-But...
John.
-Don't make me lose my temper!
Jenny sighing.
-Of course not, John...

John.
-Here are the issues on which we have to decide. Do you want to go to
Empycrist II? Do you want to go back to Planet Earth? Do you want to choose
another planet?
Paul.
-Isn't it a little bit biased, John? It is clear that you want to go to Empycrist, and
this is the first question. You are trying to influence the voters
this way, aren't you?
John.
-I am not trying anything, but it is self-evident that this is the only reasonable
option!
Peter.
-John, could you clarify a point?
What will happen

if we answer "no" each time?
John.
-There is an easy answer: in that case
I will decide!
Peter.
-What if we answer "yes"?
John.
-Don't be ridiculous; we are intelligent: we have opinions, at least I have. If you do so,
my vote will settle the matter.
Paul.
-How will we vote?
John.
-We will raise our hands.
Peter.
-Personally, I prefer a secret ballot.
John.
-It doesn't make any sense. If you have an idea and regard it as fair, you explain it and fight for it.
Paul.
-John is right; you don't have anything to hide:
we will not stone you to death!
John.
-Fine, if we all agree on everything, let's vote.

THAT IS WHAT THEY DID, and the result was not a surprise: they all agreed to continue their journey to Empycrist. Was this vote a good idea? I am not so sure: when reason reigns, whatever the parameters, the result is always the same. Hence, in the different systems of government, if the people who decide are sane and knowledgeable, they always follow the diktat of reason! It is not the same if some of them are ignorant, immature, or completely crazy. In that case, you must cross your fingers and hope that the leaders will not implement a demagogic policy and make the voters' ravings come true. Most of the time, unfortunately, they are as crazy as the citizens since they emanate from this wild logic. Bear in mind that Hitler came into power thanks to democratic elections; and look at what they did to Planet Earth: they voted in order to destroy it! Immature, unbalanced, insane, or ignorant people are unable to understand. If you allow them to take political action, they will nuke the planet. This kind of rabble must not vote!

They went back to their cabins and started to think about Empycrist. Actually, nobody has ever walked on its surface. What will they find? Is it the Promised Land they see in their dreams? The Garden of Eden is a place you build with your own hands; it is not given to you, for you don't deserve it. When you plant each tree and flower and wait for a long time in order to see the result, your dreams are rewarded with the relevance of your work. When you take care of a plant, something so different from you, you feel that you are trying to create a kind of paradise on Earth. Hush! At the moment, they are watering their dreams...

Chapter 8:
The Promised Land.

Empycrist at last! The anxious astronauts are crushed against their seats. They are about to leave the planet's orbit. Behind them, there is the terrifying darkness of outer space and in front of them the empyreal blue of Empycrit's oceans. They are about to start all over again. The human adventure is not over. Five people are going to breathe, walk, sing, paint and sow. In the greenhouse, the orange trees are blooming. There is water on Empycrist: you will drink soon. Everything is quiet; everyone is silent. Bang, bang: their hearts are beating. There will be no drums, no arrows, no war dances. Jenny is looking at the clouds. Bang, bang: this is the music of your hopes. Peter, how do you imagine the Promised Land? Green? It will be green, and blue! Paul can hardly breathe. The ground is close now. They can see grass... trees, and flowers too. Barbara is sighing. John is crying. It should have been different...

The door opens. Can you smell this? It is indescribable. It is the smell of peace. The butterflies welcome them. It is the dawn of felicity. The honey bees sing; the sun shines; time stops. They walk in the Garden of Eden. Millions of daffodils wave; billions of peonies bow. The pine trees shiver. Can you hear this sound? Birds! There are birds and they sing for you. A deer jumps into a river. Two squirrels play with a pine cone. The hinds look at them. Where are the cavemen? There is none. Where are the serpent and its apple? Here there are no apple trees, no serpents, no human beings. This is a gift from the universe, which is bestowed upon you. The sky is so blue! The grass is so green! Gaze; don't destroy! Use; don't damage! They sit down. They touch the water. The silent frogs look at them. So many miles; so much pain. I am ageless; I was born billions of years ago, and I remember... everything... Time, don't move! Let me feel this absence of pain...

Bang, bang: my heart is beating; time is moving again and the honey bees are starting to dance. Colours are exploding: Nature is blooming. Today is a good day to start to live in peace. Don't forget your past, for this original sin is the subtle pain that will prevent you from repeating the same mistakes. Man, listen to her: she is about to teach you how to become yourself. You have reached Empycrist at last: your odyssey is over. Reef the sails in, cast the anchor and **BE!**

Peter.
-I did not expect that.
John.
-I am speechless.
Paul.
-So am I.
Barbara.
-It is so...
Jenny.
-So unexpected and beautiful...
John.
-It is strange: it looks like the Earth.
Peter.
-No, it looks like the past of the Earth!
Barbara.
-Was it so...
Peter.
-Yes, it was so amazing.
John.
-But we traveled through space, not time!
Paul.
-We are not on Earth, for sure. This sun is not ours, and the planets of this
planetary system
are... different!
John.
-Different but so familiar!

Barbara.
-It doesn't make any sense.
Peter.
-It does make sense but we don't see it.
Paul.
-What is the meaning of the universe?
Jenny.
-Us!
Paul.
-I don't understand you.
Jenny.
-All this exists because we exist.
John.
-Is it a mirage, a hallucination perceived by poor thirsty fellows looking for an oasis of peace in the very middle of the desert of their sorrows?
Jenny.
-No, the exquisite, perfect mechanism works like a perpetual motion clock. Everything is automatic; even the plants and animals live a kind of automatic life, and man is inside the everlasting mechanism. Man does not dance like the other things.
Paul.
-Man cannot dance because
he is not an automaton: he thinks.
Jenny.
-So he is different from all the rest!
Paul.
-You are right Jenny: man is one of a kind. The will which created this unimaginable motion gave a part of itself – I mean its will, thinking skills and humanity – to one creature: man!
Jenny.
-The mind gives a mind to man so that he may understand everything after a titanic war against himself. If he loses this war, he fails to become a man, which turns him into a brute.
Paul.

-If he wins, he becomes a human being, acknowledges his duties and takes the lead:

he starts to create... Consciousness creates; barbarity exterminates...

John.

-But what must he create?

Jenny.

-He must create what we are going to create:

a humanized universe.

Peter.

-He must create a civilization.

Barbara.

-Are we going to do this here?

John.

-We are five!

Peter.

-We are not here for that reason.

Barbara.

-Why are we here?

Peter.

-To find ourselves. We reached the garden of consciousness and found the tree of the knowledge of... the truth!

Barbara.

-What are we going to do?

John.

-Go back!

Barbara crying.

-Everything is so much... larger than life here. Everything is perfect and... we will be happy! I don't want to go back: my husband is dead, your relatives and friends are dead...

there's nothing left.

Peter.

-Man's life is a tragedy. The birds you see and the flower you touch don't suffer
like we do.
Paul.
-They don't suffer like we do, but it seems that they expect something from us.
They are looking at us as if we were going to tell them something extraordinarily
important,
as if we had begotten them.
John.
-What will we find on Earth?
Jenny.
-Very few people.
Barbara.
-We could bring them here,
hasn't it been planned this way?
Paul.
-They must not come here. This divine perfection
is not for them; it is for us.
John.
-What will we create on Earth?
Peter.
-A kind of paradise.
John.
-What kind of paradise?
Peter.
-Something that will not look like the past.
Jenny.
-Something that could last forever.
John.
-What kind of society?
Paul.
-I don't know yet.
Barbara.
-Are there still enough people to start all over again? ... I cannot have children: I
am too old.
Jenny.

JOURNEY TO EMPYCRIST II

-I would have liked to have children.

Peter.

-I prefer other people's children. When I look at them, I don't see myself; I don't see their parents either. I just see life and the possibility of wisdom.

Barbara.

-They will have children, and I won't love them: I will raise them. I'll love them when they become human beings.

Paul.

-We will educate them; old age will sow the seeds of consciousness.

THEY LOOK AT ONE ANOTHER and don't speak anymore. The honey bees fly; the birds sing. Time, once again, seems to stop. Empycrist shines. I am hypnotized by this ethereal reality. Like the shadow puppets of an improbable pantomime, they stand up slowly and walk towards the spaceship. Barbara's blue eyes dive into the impertinent blue of the sky. Jenny sighs. Peter picks a flower; Paul touches the water again. John cries; I don't know why...

Chapter 9:
The return trip.

In the greenhouse of the Invictus, it's always spring. It is not as beautiful as Empycrist, but it is more real, even though everything is artificial. Actually, there are more imperfections here, which makes it more credible. Perfection is rare and thus almost unreal. Peter is watering the plants while Barbara is reading a book. She has left her apes alone, for I think she is beginning to realize that her researches lead nowhere.

Peter.
-Good morning, Barbara.
Barbara.
-Hi, Peter.
Peter.
-You are not with your chimpanzees:
what's going on?
Barbara.
-I am fed up. My work doesn't serve any purpose anymore. Since everything has been destroyed on Earth, I won't go back to the University of Edelpic; I won't pretend that I have discovered something extraordinary; I won't be promoted; I won't terrorize ignorant students, and I...
Well, how can I employ these monkeys?
Peter.
-Honestly, I don't know! When I was a biology student, I remember that I did not like to study mammals. Those big animals that are, most of the time, at the top of the food chain, are quite useless. Of course, monkeys disseminate the seeds of certain plants, but when you compare them with insects, you realize that without these tiny little things, life would not exist.
Barbara.

-I realize that I should have studied something else. Materialism is a dead end!

Peter.

-I am happy to hear you say that;

I am happy and surprised...

Barbara.

-By the way, I am reading a book that I have never read. It is *Alice's Adventures in Wonderland.*

Peter.

-I read it when I was a child, and I did not understand anything. Then I read it again in 11th grade, and I understood that it dealt with something essential: the eternal fight

between madness and reason.

Barbara.

-I am quite surprised. The childish creatures

that are portrayed seem so wild.

It is not a children's book.

Peter.

-In think it was first written for an adult: the author himself. Then it was turned into a children's book,

a book millions of children have read

and misunderstood!

Barbara.

-The world described is terrifying.

Peter.

-It is the world underneath your reason.

It is darkness and fear.

Barbara.

-What does the rabbit represent?

Peter.

-The time you must tame if you want to understand that your live is not eternal.
It is the noise of the clock which moves you to realize that you must hurry up,
become a sane adult
before you die, or...
Barbara.
-Or?
Peter.
-You die but you stay alive! You consciously enter the Hades of madness. You become the Queen of Hearts. You roar, you vociferate, for you suffer. Your suffering is abysmal because you know it is your fault, and your guiltiness compels you to behead.
Barbara.
-Why?
Peter.
-Because, this way, you try to gouge out the eyes that belittle you, these small mirrors
in which you see the barbarity you display.
Barbara.
-She is the devil.

Peter.
-Yes, she is.
Barbara.
-And Alice?
Peter.
-She escapes. Little Alices always grow up because they want to grow up.
Don't you think so... Alice?
Barbara.
-... Yes... I want to grow up!
Peter.
-You have changed so much... Barbara.
Barbara.
-Maybe, I don't know.

JOURNEY TO EMPYCRIST II

Peter.
-You don't know, but you feel it, don't you?
Barbara.
-... Yes... I do!

John.
-I saw Barbara this morning and
she is not the same person anymore.
Peter.
-It is clear that she has changed. She is more
mature, more intelligent, more decent.
You see, John, when reason reigns,
people can move mountains.
John.
-Does it mean that you have moved this mountain?
Peter.
-Mountains move without anybody's help.
In the end, it is the individual
who chooses to learn or not.
John.
-What happens when people don't want to learn?
Peter.
-Society must find them an appropriate place so that they may help it to survive
and prosper. At the same time they must be guided
through what they once rejected.
John.
-I am quite pessimistic about education. I remember my younger years... It was
so chaotic
that I feel certain that I learned nothing in what they used to call "high schools".
Peter.
-High schools! John, it's already too late!
You learn when you are six, not fifteen!
John.

-I remember when I was six.
Everything was new and appealing.
Peter.
-Were you scared by what you did not know?
John.
-Oh no; I wanted to see the world.
Peter.
-When you were fifteen, were you still
in a hurry to see the world?
John.
-I must say, I was more self-centered.
Peter.
-Didn't you want to be with people like you?
John.
-Maybe... But what can you teach to a child
aged six? Can you teach him or her
to be reasonable and humane?
Peter.
-Of course, you can, and it is not really difficult. When you teach them how to
read and write, you must already put emphasis on the meaning of the words and
grammatical structures. In a language, everything is meaningful. When people
understand what they write or say, it is clear that they do not react to senseless
impulses. Words and tenses are ideas; combine them and look at the result: you
enable your pupils
to become geniuses.
John.
-But drawing, or Fine Arts in general,
can serve the same purpose.
Peter.
-You are right, and it is even more evident. When a child draws the piece of
reality he has in front of him, he learns to accept it as it is.
When you copy it, you obey the truth.
John.
-But what if he changes it?
Peter.

-It depends, but if he beautifies it, this shows that he understands himself; he realizes that
goodness is the daughter of beauty.

Paul.
-I have just seen Barbara, she... there is...
I don't know... she has changed!
John.
-Isn't she more mature?
Paul.
-You are right: more mature. It is a miracle!
John.
-I assume that Peter is connected
with this miracle.
Paul.
-Peter, you must be a genius, for
the intelligence of people always
deteriorates as they get older.
Peter.
-This is true if they live alone. Loneliness is the enemy of improvement. Man is
not an island, for his strange nature compels him to learn how to become a
human being thanks to other human beings. You won't achieve that by yourself.
Actually, when a child examines the grownups' behavior, he slowly discovers
who he is and who he will become. He first notices that he is not an outgrowth
from his mother when his father tells his wife that the baby is also his son. Later,
when his teachers teach him how to spell his name, he acknowledges the subtle
difference between him and his image. At last, many years later, he becomes the
father of his own father and becomes a humane man.
Paul.
-And you turned Barbara into
this kind of individual
in such a short period of time!
Peter.

-The problem was that Barbara was alone. When people are very isolated, even though they don't seem to be in such a situation, one person can make the difference. But I did not change Barbara: we all changed her.
Paul.
-It is self-evident that during this journey
we have talked a lot to her.
Peter.
-Our reasonable minds compelled her
to become a reasonable human being.
John.
-Unless I am mistaken, if we had
left her alone, she would have
remained an old little girl!
Peter.
-It is even worse than that: she could have gone completely crazy. Pets, even when they look like human beings, are dangerous false brethren.
Paul.
-People can even feel lonelier when they hear the laments of the birds they have put in a cage.
John.
-In our new society, there will be
no more imprisoned birds.
Paul.
-Peter, I will free your orange trees...

John.
-You will do so, but, first, we will build a society in which there will be no more lonely people.

Chapter 10:
This is our home.

Two years have passed and the Earth is still there. The spinning top turns around its axis; it dances with the sun, which describes vertiginous ellipses. It is blue, but this blue is not as beautiful as the colour they saw on Empycrist II... Empycrist was like a dream and here it is a rather sad reality. They are in the cockpit. They have fastened their seat belts. They are looking at the blue sphere. They do not really want to know what they are going to find, for they already know it!

John.
-Back home!
The four of them sighing and looking at one another.
-Yes...
John.
-Before we land, I want to tell you that
whatever we find, I will make it work.

Barbara.
-We will find it hard to
cope with our memories.
Jenny.
-If life conditions are unbearable, we can take the survivors with us and go back
to Empycrist.
Barbara.
-We don't want to go back there.
John.

-No, we don't.
Barbara.
-We don't want to flee from ourselves. We must face our nature. It is time to gather stones together and build something that will last forever.
Paul.
-But the faithful died.
Barbara.
-No, we are the faithful.
Paul.
-Anyway, the Romans died.
Barbara.
-No, the Romans are still alive.
John.
-Paul, we are also the Romans: we can't help it!
Peter.
-I hope that the level of radiation
will not be too high.
Jenny.
-I hope that the water won't be polluted.
Barbara.
-I hope that we will find people, good people.
Jenny.
-I assume that they will realize that what they did was not the solution. After a war, there is always less madness in the souls of the survivors.
Peter.
-What's this?
John.
-I don't know, but... the temperature is rising!
Jenny.
-What does the computer say?
John.
-Jenny, I have disabled the speakers!
Jenny.
-Well, what does it indicate?
John.

-Who cares? We don't need artificial intelligence anymore. I shut off the autopilot.
I'm going to land this tin can.
Barbara.
-What's that?
John.
-A big noise.
Paul.
-And a violent impact too!
Don't tell me it's a meteorite again!
John.
-I am not telling you, Paul!
Paul.
-Is it a meteorite?
John.
-Kind of! I fear that it will be a risky landing.
Peter.
-John, we are going too fast.
John.
-There is not enough power to slow the spaceship down. **Emergency landing. Heads down!**
Paul.
-Not that again!
Barbara.
-History repeats itself!
Peter.
-My trees!
Barbara.
-I believe in you John!
John.
-Thank you, Barbara. **Touchdown!**

John.
-Welcome home!
Barbara.
-Thank you, John!

The spacecraft landed next to a lake. Everything is quiet. They undo their seat belts. Nobody is wounded and there is no major damage. The orange trees, in the greenhouse, have lost their white blossoms. John opens the door. They walk towards the lake. The Geiger counter doesn't show high levels of radiation. They remove their helmet. There is an intoxicating fragrance in the air. It is the scent of millions of daffodils and billions of peonies! The honeybees fly; the birds sing. Some frogs, two squirrels and a deer look at them. It's impossible! They seat down. John touches the water and a frog too: it jumps into the lake. Everything is real. He smiles; the others cry. John, it belongs to you; do you know that? Look over there: there is a tree that shivers.

John.
-Man, come here.
Man.
-Who are you?
John.
-I am John. And you, who are you?
Man.
-I am me.
John.
-Where are we?
Man.

-In a place where it is possible to live.

John.

-What happened?

Man.

-They killed one another.

John.

-Why?

Man.

-Because they didn't know themselves. Hence, they were afraid of the others and devoured what was the reflection of their ignorance.

John.

-Are they all dead?

Man.

-Yes, for ignorance exterminates.

John.

-Man, does it mean that mankind disappeared? Does it mean that I am dead? Was it the aim of the universe?

Man.

-It wasn't. The aim of the universe was you.
Thanks to your volition, you were able
to choose your own destiny.

John.

-And I chose to die!

Man.

-You did not; the monsters did so.

John.

-Man...

Man.

-Yes, John.

John.

-Who am I?

Man.

-You are the best part of the universe. You are the chef d'oeuvre of the mind that creates everything. John, you are a human being.

John speaking to himself.

-What must I do?
Man.
-Be yourself, John, and think.
Paul.
-What can we do if everybody is dead?
Jenny speaking to herself.
-What a waste!
Peter.
-Are you sure there are no other survivors?
Barbara.
-There are other survivors. The people who died were the monsters. The wise
men
and women survived.
Peter.
-Man, who are you, actually?
Barbara.
-The best part of the universe: a man blessed with reason and humanity. He is
the aim of everything, for he is a measure of nothing. He is the one who can
only be compared to himself, and, in the end, he reveals his nature by means of
his completeness. Man, let me take
your hand and take you
to the land of my human geometry.

ON THAT DAY, THE SUN was shining and the sky was bluer than the bluest blue. Barbara held the hand of this man. He took them to a village where there were quite a few inhabitants. Peter planted all his trees along the shore of the lake. Barbara freed the chimpanzees; John burned the spaceship; Jenny deleted the memories of her computer; Paul tried to forget the past: people of good will don't need history books to tell them what to do, for their futures relies on their natures.

Then came the spring of a year I will remember forever. They all took the seeds Peter had preciously kept in hundreds of small boxes, and they sowed... Nature is a brilliant painter... Some months later, the seeds gave birth to a gigantic mosaic of colours, a sea of flowers. I remember the poppies; I love poppies. I remember the sweet peas. People of good will can turn the driest deserts into promised lands. The year after, Peter's fruit trees bloomed and fructified: they ate apricots and tangerines. Wise people always plant trees, even though they are not certain that they will eat the fruit of their labor. Little by little, they gathered stones together and built. They built dams, canals, roads, bridges and houses. They rebuilt Jericho! However, this time, they did not build high walls around. They preferred to protect people from themselves; the enemy is not the human in front of you: it is your incompleteness. Hence, they clipped the claws of the tiger and gave him a heart, for they gave him a mind. How did they achieve what a million years had not achieved? It is simple: they enabled people to think. Man started to think, and he started to create.

In the beginning, unique and eternal, there was the mind that conceives. Then came the Age of Lead, a time of darkness, cruelty and sorrow, but man decided to become a creature that thinks...

74

By the way,

can

you

think?